Trumping Trouser Trev

Written by Bonnie Reynolds
Illustrated by Sarah Waterfield

AuthorHouse™ UK
1663 Liberty Drive
Bloomington, IN 47403 USA
www.authorhouse.co.uk
Phone: 0800.197.4150

Published by AuthorHouse 01/11/2016

ISBN: 978-1-5049-9786-7 (sc)
ISBN: 978-1-5049-9787-4 (e)

authorHOUSE®

Trumping Trouser Trevor

Have you ever wondered when you lie in bed,
Of what may happen while you sleep,
While you drift away to the land of nod
Carried to your slumber deep?

Are you nestled comfortably, tucked up in your bed?
Ready for the story to fill you dreamy head,
With images of magic, excitement and wonder too,
then listen little one,
As this tale I tell to you!

Now this tale tells of the queer little life
Of a pixie of the rudest sort,
His round barrel belly stuff tight in his pants
And cheeks the colour of Port!
His hair was a mass of ginger curls
That bounced on his head like springs
And his bottom wobbled as he walked
That's what eating too many doughnuts brings!

Now you'd think his mother would see that his clothes
Were fit for a child half his age
And that his belly would blubber and bounce around
Like a wild beast trapped in a cage!

Now this little Pixie known only to us
As Trumping Trouser Trevor
Was well known for varied 'Trouser Songs'
That he thought incredibly clever!

Trumping Trouser Trevor would wander around
The joys of life clearly filling his heart
Even his cheery face and jovial song
Couldn't excuse his triumphant FARTS!

People would look and recoil in horror
Holding the nose on the front of their face,
Could that big noise have come from a boy?
He was a terrible Pixie disgrace!!

But the pixie would just skip and giggle and laugh
Knowing the shock that his bottom would cause,
Before saving and brewing the best one he had
Releasing the tremendous 'Trouser Applause'

Now this fart rattled and rang through streets
Crowds of people the gross smell it parted,
The people had long stopped blaming to dogs,
They knew that Trevor had farted!
What would become of this Trouser Belcher?
Whose fumes turned the Pixie air blue,
He was fast becoming a Pixie concern,
What were the Pixies to do?

For he spent all his days loitering around the bakers,
Ready for a fresh batch of cake,
Once consumed the baker would brace himself
For a trump that would make the shelves shake!

And as sure as you like Trevor's bottom, it shouted,
Sounding like ten slippery seals clapping
This just was no good; something had to be done,
Shouted the baker 'HE NEEDS HIS KNUCKLES WRAPPING'
But surely this habit the poor boy had
Must have some use to his kind,
For he thought his Trouser burps were just brill,
A solution they just had to find!

And so comes the old Pixie, the wise man of their kind
And gathers the elders of the land,
Could he have a solution to the very smelly problem?
That was polluting the quaint Pixie land?
In a croaky old Pixie voice he began
'an idea I may av thus far'
'ow bout we get Trumping Trouser Trev
To funnel his farts in to a jar'

A puzzled look fell upon all the faces
Of the other Elder pixies congregated,
What good could this mean to Trevor and his bottom?
An explanation they all awaited!
'Well see, them fumes that come from his bum
When ignited could light a furnace,
So ow bout we pipe it straight to the bakers
Then is bum would be of a service'

'Weems could get him a teacher while his farts they brewed
So educated and clever eed become'
And when he felt one coming he could shut himself away,
Sending the gases to down the funnel from his bum'
"Thems would keep the baker's ovens lit" he said
"For an eternity, if not more"
"And keep his mother in free doughnuts and bread
And puddings forever more"

The Elders agreed this was surely a plan,
That could leave the Pixies air clean,
And for Trevor to be taught and eat all he can
Would surely be a heavenly dream!

When the solution was told to Trumping Trouser Trev,
Well, his trousers he darn nearly split um
Overwhelmed with excitement I'm sure a button popped
He'd surely now need a new pair that fit him

And so there we are, Trumping Trouser Trev,
Went from disgrace to Pixie Eco Prince,
Although the rumour has it, doughnuts have been replaced
With pies full of custard and mince!
Now little children as you drift off to sleep,
Remember, we're ALL full of smelly bottom gasses,
But just like Trumping Trouser Trevor,
Try your best in all of your classes!!